THREE GOLDEN ORANGES

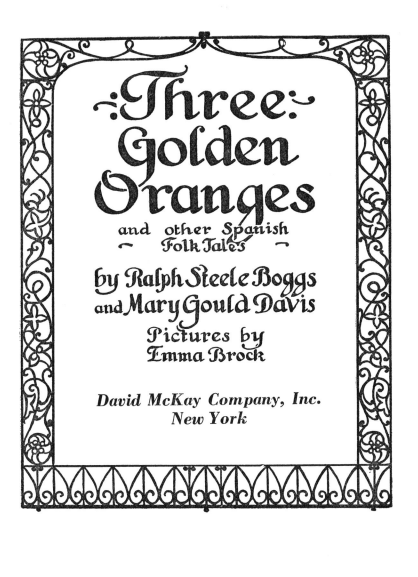

Three Golden Oranges

and other Spanish Folk Tales

by Ralph Steele Boggs
and Mary Gould Davis

Pictures by
Emma Brock

David McKay Company, Inc.
New York

For

RALPH KARL BOGGS

FOREWORD

THESE tales truly represent the oral tradition of Spain and the color of her countryside, from the green, moist mountains of Asturias and the barren brown plateaux of Castilla to the shady gardens and snow-capped peaks of Andalusia.

From several hundred native folk tales, found in various collections and gathered at first hand, the present selection has been made. These stories were told to the collector by the people themselves. They were written in their present form under Spanish skies, often in cities and villages that were the actual places of their origin. The artist who drew the pictures sat on bare, sunny hillsides near Granada, on the quais beside the river at Cadiz, and in the sheltered coolness of the Alcazar gardens in Seville reproducing with her pencil the scenes that are the natural background for these tales.

No one can travel very far over the roads of Spain

and not feel that her people are brimming over with stories, stories that have been told for centuries and that have never yet found their way between the covers of a book. Spain is, as a country, too individual, too reticent to be easily understood by a stranger. To know her folk tales and her music is to understand her better. To trace them along her dusty roads, through her olive groves and old walled cities, over her wide plains and fertile valleys, on and up into the splendid heights of the Sierra Nevada is a revealing adventure.

The three people who have made this book have had that adventure. What they found in Spain they pass on to you.

CONTENTS

ILLUSTRATIONS

was fair, with hair as golden as ripe corn, and her blue eyes looked frightened. Diego made her his most graceful bow.

"Can you tell me," he said, "where I shall find the Garden of the Three Golden Oranges?"

The girl shook her head.

"I do not know," she answered. "My father is the Sun and he may know. He will be home very soon now, but you must go away before he comes. He will be very angry if he finds you here."

But Diego laughed and refused to go. He followed the girl into the Castle of the Sun and talked to her so charmingly that she forgot her fear and became as gay and happy as a child. Suddenly a deep golden light flooded the room and the Sun himself stood in the doorway.

"Who is this stranger, my daughter?" he demanded. "Let him explain himself or it will be the worse for you both."

The frightened look came back into the girl's eyes.

"Father," she said, "he means no harm. He seeks the Garden of the Three Golden Oranges. Can you tell him where it is?"

The Sun shook his great head.

"I do not know," he said. "Let him go still higher

and ask my sister, the Moon.   And let him go quickly before I lose my temper."

Bidding farewell to the daughter of the Sun, Diego hurried to the great gate which opened silently to let him through.   On and upward he went, following the curves of the road ever higher and higher.   At last he saw on the slope above him a Castle that was made of silver.   Like the Castle of the Sun it had a great wrought iron gate, and when Diego rang the bell the gate swung open.   On the path that led to the door of the Castle there stood a tall young girl.   Her hair was so fair that it looked like silver and her eyes were gray.

"Can you tell me," said Diego, not forgetting to bow, "where I shall find the Garden of the Three Golden Oranges?"

The girl shook her head.

"I do not know," she answered, "but I will ask my mother, the Moon."

She went quickly into the Castle from which a silvery light shone.   Presently she returned.

"You are to go at once," she told Diego.   "Go along the road until you come to a Castle that is built of gray rock.   There dwells my uncle, the East Wind.   He blows everywhere, all over the world, and surely he will know where your Garden is to be found."

Diego thanked her and started out again. He was tired and hungry, his throat was dry with the white dust, before he saw above him the great gray Castle of the East Wind. Again he rang a bell and again a great gate swung open. The girl who stood on the pathway this time was so pretty that Diego's heart beat faster. Her brown eyes were bright with mischief and she wore a red carnation in her dark hair.

"You are a very foolish youth to come here," she told him. "If my father, the East Wind, sees you he will probably blow you over the top of the Sierra Nevada."

"Perhaps it is there that I want to go," Diego answered boldly. "I am seeking the Garden of the Three Golden Oranges. Do you know where it lies?"

The girl raised her black eyebrows.

"Why should I bother to know that?" she said. "My father knows, of course. He knows everything. If you will entertain me all the afternoon, if you will eat with me and drink with me and tell me about the world below the mountains, I will hide you in the chest beside the fireplace when my father comes home. Then I will ask him where this Garden is, and you can listen to his answer. And if you are brave and clever you can get away without his seeing you."

The hours of the day passed very quickly for them

both. The daughter of the East Wind was so charmin that Diego forgot his quest and thought only of her. Was she, perhaps, the most beautiful girl in all the world?

Toward night there was a great clatter and bustle in the courtyard, and a chill wind blew in through doors and windows.

"That is my father," said the girl quickly. "Go and hide in the chest beside the fireplace."

Diego crouched down inside the great chest and the girl threw over it a gaily embroidered blanket. "Now listen well," she whispered.

Presently Diego heard the East Wind come into the room. In spite of his rough manners he seemed to be a kindly person. He pinched his daughter's cheek and pulled a lock of her dark hair.

"And what have you been doing today while I have been blowing my way across the world?" he asked.

His daughter seemed not at all afraid of him. "Father," she said, "I have a question to ask you. Where lies the Garden of the Three Golden Oranges?"

The East Wind laughed until the great wooden rafters shook. "Now what care have you for the Three Golden Oranges?" he shouted. "That is a quest for a man, not for a woman. The Garden lies just on the other side of the crest of the highest peak in the Sierra Nevada. If you stand on the top you can look down and see the Garden and the Orange Tree below you. But enough of this chatter! I am hungry. Bring me meat and drink!"

That night while East Wind slept Diego made his way out of the Castle, the gate opening silently to let him through. All that day and the next day, and the next and the next, he worked his way up the highest peak of the Sierra Nevada, through fields starred with wild flowers, through drifts of snow. There was no sound in his ears but the lonely cry of a bird or the trickle of the clear, cold stream. He seemed quite alone in a strange, silent world.

At dawn on the fifth day he stood on the crest of the highest peak, and looking down, he saw the Garden.

Surely it was the loveliest Garden in all the world. It was like an emerald set in the snow. Tall cypress trees guarded it, roses and lilies and carnations bloomed, fountains threw up their sparkling jets of water. And in the center of the Garden there stood an Orange Tree. Even from his height Diego could see that only three oranges grew on its branches and that these three shone and glistened like the purest gold.

Eagerly he ran down the slope and rang the bell in

the Garden wall, and silently the gate swung open. It
was very still in the Garden and there was no living
soul in sight. Diego went up to the tree. Remember-
ing what the wise woman had said, he did not try to
climb it, but leaped in the air until he had leaped high
enough to catch the branch that bore the fruit. Quickly
he broke it off. They were his, the Three Golden
Oranges!

Thrusting them into his pouch, he hurried through
the Garden to the gate. Would it open for him? For
an instant he waited, listening. Then the gate swung
silently open, and he was free. Wrapping his cloak
about him he slept. And the next day he started on
his homeward journey.

If the way to the Garden had seemed long, the way
back seemed even longer. One day when Diego could
see below him the white roofs and square red towers of
Granada he sat down to rest beside the road. His
mouth was so parched with thirst that he took from his
pouch one of the Three Golden Oranges. He looked
at it longingly.

"It could do no harm," he said to himself, "if I ate
just one of them."

He broke the skin of the orange — and out of it there
stepped a tiny maiden!

In the center of the garden there stood an orange tree

Slender and delicate, just as tall as his little finger, she stood there on the palm of his hand. My, but she was lovely! Her eyes were as bright as the stars in a June sky, her hair was as black as a crow's wing, her curved mouth as red as a passion flower. Her long, ruffled dress was of yellow muslin and on her tiny arched feet she wore golden shoes.

Light as thistle-down, she sprang from Diego's hand to the ground. And there she stood — as tall as he!

Diego could only stand and gape at her. Surely this was the most beautiful girl in all the world!

Lifting her yellow fan so that it hid her lips, she looked at him over its rim.

"Will you give me some bread?" she asked.

Diego was so dazed with her beauty that he could only answer stupidly, "I have none."

"Then," said the girl, "I will creep back into my Golden Orange and return to my tree."

With that she became small again and curled up inside the orange. And both girl and orange disappeared.

Now Diego had a head on his shoulders and you must know by this time that he was not easily discouraged. He felt in his pouch to be sure that the other two oranges were there. Then he went on until he came to a goatherd's hut, where he begged a piece of bread. Sitting down on the hillside under an olive tree, he took the second Golden Orange from his pouch and broke the skin. And out there stepped a second maiden. My, but she was lovelier than the first!

Her hair was as gold as the flowers of the broom, her eyes as blue as the wild lupin and her lips like the curved petals of a pink rose. Her long, ruffled dress was of blue and her shoes were silver.

Lightly she leaped to the ground, and there she stood just as high as Diego's shoulder.

"Will you give me some bread?" she asked, resting the edge of her fan against her lips.

Diego took the bread from his pouch and handed it to her.

"And now," she said, "will you give me some water?"

Diego's heart sank.

"I have none," he answered.

"Then," said the girl, "I will creep back into my little Orange and return to my tree."

And with that she grew small again, curled up inside the orange skin, and girl and orange disappeared.

And now Diego wished that he had heeded the words of the old wise woman and had brought the oranges to her. But something made him feel that he would like to finish the adventure for himself. So he walked to where a brook flowed down the hillside. Taking the bread from his pouch he laid it on the grass beside him and opened the third Golden Orange.

My, but the tiny maiden who stepped out of this one was the loveliest of all! Diego knew now that he had found the most beautiful girl in all the world!

Her hair, under the black lace mantilla, was red gold, she had the long gray eyes of Andalusia and her eyebrows and lashes were as black as night. Her dress was snow white, the many ruffles edged with scarlet, and on her slender feet she wore scarlet shoes. When she jumped to the ground she stood just as high as Diego's heart.

"Will you give me some bread?" she asked, her eyes smiling at him over her scarlet fan.

Diego's fingers trembled with eagerness as he gave her the bread.

"And now," she said, "will you give me some water?"

He scooped the clear water from the brook and gave it to her.

"And now," she said, "we will eat together and drink together and live happily ever afterward."

Diego's heart leaped with joy. They ate and drank, and then, with the girl's cool hand clasped in his, her white skirts rustling crisply as she walked, they went on down the road toward Granada.

Just before they reached the town they passed an Inn. In the patio there was a fountain and over the basin of the fountain there grew an olive tree.

"See," said the girl, "you cannot bring your bride into Granada on foot. Go into the Inn and ask them to let you have a carriage and a pair of horses. Bargain well for it, and I will wait for you up in the olive tree."

And with that she climbed up into the tree and settled down there, looking for all the world like a great scarlet and white bird.

Diego went on into the Inn, and what with bargaining with the shrewd landlord for a carriage and pair, and celebrating the happy ending of his quest with a glass or two of *valdepeñas,* it was some time before he came out again.

No sooner had he disappeared than out of the shadow of the wall there came a woman dressed as a gypsy. And how was the gray-eyed girl to know that she was really a wicked witch? As the gypsy bent over to fill her pitcher at the fountain she saw the face of the girl reflected in the water, and jealousy of the beauty of that face filled her.

She lifted the pitcher and threw it into the basin

"If that face were mine," she thought, "there would be no end to my power."

Long she looked at the reflected face, and then, in a frenzy of rage, she lifted the pitcher and threw it into the basin, thus breaking both the pitcher and the reflection. Now, for her own purposes, the witch was acting as a servant at the Inn. When she came back without the pitcher, the Innkeeper gave her another one and told her, impatiently, to fill that. For the second time she saw the reflected face, and for the second time in her rage she destroyed both pitcher and image. This time when she returned to the kitchen with empty hands the Innkeeper scolded her soundly. Then he gave her a pitcher that was made of metal. In a frenzy the witch banged it against the fountain, but it would not break.

Up in the olive tree the gray-eyed girl of the third Golden Orange laughed at her.

This, to the witch, was the last straw. Climbing the tree as swiftly as a cat she stuck a magic pin into the girl's head. And there in the branches of the olive tree sat, not a gray-eyed maiden, but a little white dove.

When Diego came out of the Inn and discovered that the most beautiful girl in all the world had disappeared, he was distracted. Vainly he hunted for her through the Inn and the orchard and along the road. Then he threw himself in despair on the grass under the olive and mourned aloud, while his mourning was echoed by the plaintive cry of the white dove in the branches above him. Finally Diego drew the dove down and held it against his breast.

"Come with me, little dove," he said. "Together we will go to the wise woman and ask her how I can find my lost love."

For days and for weeks the old wise woman had sat at the entrance of her cave and watched for Diego. And now she saw him coming, his face sad and downcast, the glistening white dove held against his breast.

And instantly, in her wisdom, she knew what had happened. And her anger at the witch, who was in truth her enemy, made her old eyes glow like live coals. Stretching out her hands she took the dove from Diego without a word. Her thin, brown fingers felt about under its feathers and touched almost at once the head of the magic pin. Swiftly she drew it out — and there before them stood the gray-eyed girl of the third Golden Orange!

Gratefully Diego thanked the wise old woman, proudly he led his bride to his mother's house. A fine pair they made, standing before the altar. The wedding festivities lasted three days and three nights. I, myself, was there as a guest. And I came away with nothing in my pouch but the skin of a golden orange.

TÍO PACO AND HIS WONDERFUL DONKEY

TÍO PACO AND HIS WONDERFUL
DONKEY

IN THE little town of Carmona not far from Seville, there once lived an old peasant who was known to his neighbors as Tío Paco. That was not, of course, the name given to him by the *cura* at the baptismal font, but long before he reached middle age it was the name that everyone used.

And it suited him. In all the four kingdoms of

Andalusia it would be difficult to find a more innocent or a more gullible man. He was, moreover, kind and merry and on good terms with everyone. His father had left him a small white-washed house, a garden and a fine grove of olive trees. His children were all grown up and married, his wife was a good manager, and the two of them lived throughout the year in great happiness and contentment.

Now Tío Paco had a donkey of whom he was exceedingly fond, so fond, in fact, that he was inclined to do the donkey's work as well as his own. Pedro, for that was the donkey's name, carried the fruit and vegetables to market, it is true; but instead of riding him as most peasants ride their donkeys, Tío Paco trudged along beside him, holding the bridle over his arm. He tried to persuade himself that this was because he was getting too fat and needed the exercise. But it really was because of his deep affection for Pedro, who was, it must be admitted, an unusually fine donkey.

In the first place, Pedro's coat was white — there was not a gray hair, a black hair nor a brown hair on it. Tío Paco was so proud of this coat that he did not shave Pedro as most men shave their donkeys. He let the ivory white coat grow long and thick, cutting it only where the saddle rested. And if Pedro was a little too warm on the long summer days, his own pride in his coat was so great that he did not resent it. In the second place Pedro was intelligent — very intelligent. Tío Paco talked to him as he would talk to a man. And by a certain twitching of his ear and a knowing roll of his eyes, Pedro answered him.

One fine morning in May Tío Paco filled Pedro's baskets with fruit and vegetables from the garden and set out for the market. As usual, he walked holding the halter over his arm. Now there was in Carmona at this time a group of poor students who were supposed to study every day with the priests in the monastery. Often they had seen Tío Paco and Pedro pass the cloisters where their classes were held in warm weather, and they knew both of Tío Paco's gullibility and of his affection for his donkey. On this particular morning they had determined to play a trick upon him and to win the donkey for their own gain.

As Tío Paco passed they called out to him. Always ready to chat, merry and sociable, Tío Paco let the halter lie slack on his arm while he told for the boys' benefit his best and most amusing stories. He was fond of making gestures, and in one of his movements the halter slipped from his arm and fell to the roadway.

Very quietly one of the students crept up behind him

and led Pedro away. Very swiftly he transferred the baskets to his own back and the halter to his own neck. And a few minutes later when, feeling a twitch of the reins, Tío Paco turned, he found at the end of them not his donkey but a young and handsome student!

Tío Paco's amazement knew no bounds. His mouth fell open, his eyes stared.

"Holy Mother of God!" he cried. "What is this?"

The student, who had rehearsed his part well, rolled his large brown eyes very much as Pedro had rolled his, and answered in low, humble tones:

"Tío Paco, have mercy upon me! Listen to my story! I have been an idle and mischievous boy, a good-for-nothing. Often my father has said to me, 'You are too stupid and too obstinate to be human. You are as dull and as stubborn as a donkey!' On a certain day four years ago he said it once too often, and a donkey I became. No sooner did the words leave my father's lips than down on all fours I went without being able to help myself, a tail appeared and my ears grew long. When I tried to speak I could do nothing but bray. Fortunately for me, it was you who bought me, Tío Paco. You have been a kind master to me. Often I have felt indeed that you knew a human soul dwelt in your Pedro's body. But now, after four years, my father must have repented and prayed the good God to restore me to my human form. You have witnessed a miracle, Tío Paco. Forgive me all the trouble I have caused you, and let me go and find my father."

Now there are some men in Andalusia who would have detected this trick and found this sad tale hard to credit. But Tío Paco, being what he was, believed every word of it. He reassured the student, congratulated him upon the miracle and, taking the halter from his neck and the basket from his back, bade him go freely and with his blessing.

In the days that followed Tío Paco sadly missed his clever donkey. He dared not tell his wife and the neighbors what had become of Pedro because the student had assured him that if the story became known, his life would be made unbearable to him. So Tío Paco explained the disappearance of his donkey with this story and that story. And the neighbors shook their heads and significantly tapped their foreheads, and firmly believed that the loss was entirely due to his innocence and gullibility — which indeed it was.

The weeks went by, and it was time for the annual Fair at Mairena. Tío Paco and his wife filled the baskets of the new, and ordinary, donkey with fresh fruit and vegetables and started early for the little town. It was late in June and the white road that wound among the hills was bordered with yellow broom. The fields were bright with scarlet poppies and golden buttercups and the deep blue of wild lupin.

The road was gay with the procession making its way to Mairena — men and women and children, on donkey-back, on horse-back and on foot; pretty girls with a red carnation fastened behind their left ear; bare-footed boys driving herds of goats; even a drove of small, black pigs, grunting and squealing as they were urged along by their master. Tío Paco was one with the gay crowd, calling a cheery answer to the questions that were shouted to him. But through it all he was conscious of a feeling of loneliness, of a longing for Pedro.

"Is it not enough," he told himself sternly, "to know that the poor boy is at last restored to his own form? Can you not comfort yourself with the thought that your donkey is no longer a donkey, but a human soul?"

But in spite of this philosophy his thoughts dwelt wistfully on his vanished donkey.

Just before they reached Mairena the procession passed an encampment of gypsies under the trees beside the road. The gypsies themselves were grouped around a fire, where one of the women was stirring a pot of stew. Near-by was the wagon, covered with brown canvas, and, under a far tree, there stood a white donkey.

Tío Paco's eyes fell upon him. A white donkey — a donkey with never a gray hair, a brown hair nor a black hair in his coat, a donkey so like the lost Pedro that it might have been his twin!

To the amazement of his wife and the neighbors, Tío Paco threw himself from the back of his ordinary donkey and ran across the field.

"Pedro!" he cried.

The white donkey raised his head. His ears twitched, his eyes rolled knowingly. Tío Paco threw his arms around the shaggy neck.

"My poor, poor lad!" he said. "Have you been up to your old tricks again?   Has your father in his anger again put the curse upon you?   Are you again not a man, but a donkey?"

Pedro, for it was indeed Pedro, twitched his ears and rolled his eyes knowingly. The gypsies, who had bought him from the clever student, had treated him none too well and he was glad to see his old master.

Tío Paco stroked the moist nose.

"Never mind," he said.   "I will bargain for you with

the gypsies. You shall come home with me, and perhaps if you are a good donkey the gracious Lord will make you again a man."

Tío Paco was as good as his word. Shrewdly he bargained with the gypsies for Pedro, proudly he led him home. And if the neighbors nodded and winked and tapped their foreheads significantly, Tío Paco was too happy to care.

And as the peaceful weeks went by, "You are a good donkey," he would say to Pedro. "Why then do you not become a man?"

And Pedro would twitch his ears and roll his eyes knowingly.

Not in all the four kingdoms of Andalusia was there so petted and pampered a donkey.

white under it.   Even in midsummer, the snow clothed
them.

Toñino walked on slowly, the tunes that he had
played still singing themselves in his head, his eyes
drinking in the beauty of the night.   On the slope of
the hill, on a little raised terrace, there stood an olive
tree, old and gnarled, its leaves silvery white in the
moonlight.   Just above it, Toñino sat down on the
short, dry grass, took off his cap, and let the cool night
wind blow through his hair.   It had been a long hot
day and a long evening, and Toñino was tired.   Letting
his limbs relax, he rested his head on one outflung arm
and went to sleep.

When he awoke the moon had disappeared and the
stars blazed low and bright in the sky.   Through the
stillness there came to Toñino a faint thread of song.
At first it was only music.   Then, thin and clear, he
heard the words:

> *"Lunes y martes y miércoles tres,*
> *Lunes y martes y miércoles tres."*

Now Toñino knew the air — old and wild and filled
with an irresistible rhythm.   He raised himself on his
elbow.   Down below him on the terrace under the

olive trees the fairies were dancing. There were hundreds of them, tiny fairy men and fairy women. With heads lifted and hands joined they were dancing in a circle around the old tree, flinging their legs high in the air, their tilted, impish faces white in the starlight.

They were so intent on their dance, so lost in the rhythm of their song that they did not even see Toñino. He stared at them in delight and wonder. Often he had heard of the fairies, but never before had he seen them, and their wild grace enchanted him.

> *"Lunes y martes y miércoles tres,*
> *Lunes y martes y miércoles tres,"*

— round and round and round the tree, until Toñino grew dizzy with it!

"Hold, my little masters. If you do not know the rest of the song, I will give you a hint of it."

Lifting his guitar, he swept his fingers over the strings and sang in his full, clear voice:

> *"Lunes y martes y miércoles tres,*
> *Jueves y viernes y sábado seis!"*

The fairies shouted with joy, and instantly their tiny voices took up the words, singing in unison with Toñino

Lifting his guitar, he swept his fingers over the strings

and his guitar until the valley and the surrounding hills rang with the song.

"Lunes y martes y miércoles tres,
Jueves y viernes y sábado seis,"

— higher and shriller and sweeter until the very stars seemed to sing with them.

Suddenly the song ceased, the circle was broken and the fairies, one and all, ran up the slope to Toñino. They swarmed all over and about him, clinging to his fingers with their tiny hands, peering at him with mischievous, slanting eyes.

"A reward, Toñino! A reward!" they cried. "Make a wish and we will grant it!"

Toñino chuckled. "I want no reward, little masters," he answered. "It is enough to have seen you and to have sung with you."

But the fairies insisted. "Make a wish," they shouted. "Any wish. And we will grant it."

Toñino thought for a moment. "There is this hump of mine," he said quaintly. "It is a burden to carry, and it aches when the weather is cold. Could you take it away from me?"

Instantly a thousand little hands were laid on his back and shoulders. His body felt lifted and lightened

A white dawn mist rose from the valley and eddied about him.   Through it, ever fainter and sweeter, came the fairy voices:

"Lunes y martes y miércoles tres,
Jueves y viernes y sábado seis." . . .

Toñino rose to his feet, as straight and strong in body as he was blithe in spirit.

There was much excitement among the cave-dwellers in Granada when Toñino's tale was told.   Nothing else was talked about for days.   No one grudged him his good fortune.   And everywhere he went the eyes of the pretty girls of Granada followed him.

Now in a near-by village there lived another hunch-back boy whose name was Miguel.   He was as cross and resentful as Toñino was merry and forgiving.   To him life itself was as great a burden as the hump that he carried upon his shoulders.   He had hated Toñino always for his brave spirit, and now that he stood as tall and straight as any man, he hated him more than ever.   In his harsh, complaining voice he questioned Toñino, who told him every word of the story.   He even took him to the hillside and pointed out the ancient olive tree standing alone on its circular terrace.

"Try it, Miguel," he urged.   "Listen carefully to

the fairies first so that you surely get the air and the rhythm of their song.   And then sing with them.   Perhaps they will take your hump away, too."

That next night Miguel went out alone to the slope above the olive tree, and waited for the fairies.   And as they had come to Toñino, so they came to him.   He could see them dancing around the tree in a circle.   He could hear the thin, sweet voices:

> *"Lunes y martes y miércoles tres,*
> *Jueves y viernes y sábado seis."*

Too stupid to catch the lilt of the song, and too impatient to wait until he did, Miguel — thinking that he was being very clever — shouted abruptly:

> *"Y domingo siete!"*

Now this was a double insult to the fairies.   It rudely broke the rhythm of their stong, and it named that forbidden thing — a holy day.

With a shrill cry of scorn and rage they swarmed upon Miguel.   From some hidden place they dragged out Toñino's hump and fastened it upon his own. With pointed, impish fingers they poked and pried him, their light voices mocking him, their long, pale eyes flashing into his. It was a nightmare to Miguel, and he never quite knew how it ended.

When dawn came he found himself sitting on the hillside under the old olive tree, with two humps instead of one upon his shoulders. Never again did he try to see the fairies, and no word of his adventure ever passed his lips. To all questions he shook his head. Only Toñino guessed what had happened when Miguel added the last and unwelcome line to the fairies' song.

DON DEMONIO'S MOTHER-IN-LAW

DON DEMONIO'S MOTHER-IN-LAW

ONCE upon a time there lived in the little village of La Zubia a widow woman who was known for her long tongue and her short temper. She was thin and brown, her face and body as dried up as a piece of *esparto* grass. Her voice was as shrill as a cricket's chirp, and her tongue as sharp as a butcher's knife on market day. From the hour when God hung out the daylight till the hour when He drew it in again she was never still.

Now Tía Pía, as she was known to her neighbors, had one daughter who was pretty to look at but so lazy that even an earthquake would not move her. Her name was Pánfila, and what she liked to do best was to put on her dress of red and white muslin and sit, with folded hands, in the window, waiting for a lover to come and marry her. Every handsome youth who passed that way was a possible husband to Pánfila. And more than one of them looked back over his shoulder at her demure face and dark, carefully dressed hair. But when old Tía Pía poked her head around the doorway, each one made off as fast as he could go. Pánfila was not worth the risk of having such a one for a mother-in-law!

Day after day Pánfila sat and looked out the window, and day after day Tía Pía scolded her roundly for her idleness. Wielding her broom vigorously and raising a cloud of dust with every stroke, she would say:

"In my day girls did their share of the work of the house." Swish, swish, went the broom! "They did not sit idle with folded hands." Swish, swish! "They did not waste the good daylight waiting for fortune to come to them." Swish, swish! "They thought of something besides a possible sweetheart." Swish, swish! "The sweetheart who comes to such as you will be a good-for-nothing." Swish, swish!

One day Tía Pía called to Pánfila to help her lift from the fire a pot of hot lye. Now it may have been that Tía Pía was too quick in her movements, or it may have been that Pánfila's mind was on a handsome youth who had passed the door that morning and had been frightened away by her mother's voice. Whatever the reason, the pot of lye slipped, and a bit of the hot liquid splashed on Tía Pía's foot. You could have heard her screeching half a mile away!

"It is all your fault," she stormed. "Lazy, worthless creature. You are not worth your salt. You think of nothing but sweethearts! May you marry the Devil himself and be done with it!"

Now not long after this a young stranger appeared in the village of La Zubia. He was tall and dark, courtly in manner and obviously well off in this world's goods. Over his shoulders he wore a long cape of scarlet silk, and on his head a curious draped cap that no one ever saw him without. He said that he was a traveller from a far country, and he lost no time in making himself popular among the men of the village. The young men were willing enough to be friends with him. He evidently knew a thing or two, and no one need give his own *céntimos* for a glass of *valdepeñas* when the stranger was in the village Inn! But the old men were less easily won. They muttered among themselves and shook their heads.

"There is something queer about him," said old Tío

Blas. "His manners are too good and his hands are too white, and I don't like the look in his eyes."

"He doesn't know a lamb from a kid," muttered old Tío Gil. "He has never been near the church since he came. I saw him hide himself in a doorway the other night when the *cura* went by."

But in spite of this gossip, the stranger, who called himself Don Demonio, became a familiar figure in the village. And in no time at all Pánfila, from her window, had fallen in love with him. At first it was only a glance and a smile and a slight gesture of the hand. But Don Demonio, unlike the others, soon showed that he had no fear of old Tía Pía. Her shrill voice seemed only to amuse him, her ugly, wrinkled face to draw his eyes. His manner to her was as courtly as always, and he showered compliments upon her as extravagant as those that he paid Pánfila. By Corpus Christi Day the affair was settled and the marriage arranged.

Now old Tía Pía was as shrewd as she was ugly. She had not forgotten the wish that she had made for Pánfila when the hot lye fell on her toes. Neither was she at all sure that the draped scarlet silk of Don Demonio's cap did not conceal horns! When the wedding day arrived, she called Pánfila to her and said:

"There is one thing that you must surely do. When you are alone with your husband, see that every door and window is securely locked. See that every crack and cranny in the walls is covered. Cover the chimney, even, leave free only the keyhole of the door. Then take an olive branch that has been blessed by the *cura* and switch your husband with it. This is what all brides must do to show that they rule in the home."

Pánfila, who was a meek creature, promised. And the wedding was celebrated with much feasting and rejoicing.

Now the house that Don Demonio had prepared for Pánfila was just outside the village on the road to Granada. When the bride and groom had entered it, no one noticed old Tía Pía stealing along the side of the road with a small, empty glass bottle in her hand.

Inside the house Pánfila had carefully done all that her mother had told her to do. And, having shut the house up as tight as a drum and taken the key from the keyhole, she turned to her husband with the blessed olive branch in her hand. The instant he saw it he went, to her amazement, into a panic of fear and tried to get out of the house. Cringing and whining and begging, his courtly manners completely forgotten, he desperately sought some way of escape, while Pánfila,

no longer wondering but now suspicious, followed him
about with the olive branch.   But there was no way out
for Don Demonio excepting through the keyhole.   And
he was finally forced to take that way.   Driven to it,

he at last assumed his own form with the tail and the
horns that were rightly his, but he was no higher than
a man's little finger!   Through the keyhole he slipped
before Pánfila's astonished eyes — only to find himself
inclosed in a glass bottle!

Old Tía Pía chuckled to herself as she firmly forced in the cork.

"This is one of the times," she said, "when the Devil himself was no match for a woman."

The very next morning old Tía Pía, leaving Pánfila alternately weeping and gazing out the window for another suitor, put the bottle in her pocket, mounted on her donkey, and set out for the Sierra Nevada. It is a long ride to Monte Mulhacén, which is the highest mountain in Spain and is covered with snow the whole year round. But Tía Pía took it, every foot of the way. And there on the top of the mountain she buried the bottle deep in the snow — an element which must have been quite new to His Satanic Majesty. Then she went back to La Zubia.

Ten years went by — ten years of peace and prosperity for the world. Wives were patient and long-suffering toward their husbands, husbands tender and indulgent toward their wives, children so good that they might have been angels already. Only the lawyers were unhappy, because no man sued his neighbor and time hung heavy on their hands.

Now there passed through the village of La Zubia a gallant soldier of fortune whose name was Ricardo. He chanced to ask his way of old Tía Pía, who still wielded her broom and her tongue as briskly as ever although Pánfila had long ago married and gone to live in Córdoba. Sharp as her tongue still was, Tía Pía found that she had met her match in Ricardo, who, when she told him that his road lay over the mountains, answered cheerfully:

"If the mountains are in my way, old woman, I will ride over them even though I crack my head against Heaven's arch."

Now this was an answer that met with Tía Pía's approval, and after a dialogue that left them both breathless, they parted good friends.

Ricardo made his way up the steep, winding *cañada* that led to the top of the mountain. At the top he unsaddled his horse so that it could rest and crop the short grass, and threw himself down under a stunted tree. As he sat there idly, he saw something gleam at his feet. Stooping, he picked up a small glass bottle. Moreover, something inside the bottle moved!

"Now," said Ricardo aloud, "what strange, black insect is this?"

To his surprise a voice — a rather thin and weak voice it is true, but unquestionably a voice — answered from the bottle:

"It is no insect," said this voice. "But an honorable

and worthy devil, who, owing to the unnatural cunning of his mother-in-law, has been shut up in this bottle and buried in this most hateful of elements for ten years. Free me, good soldier, and I will grant you your heart's desire."

"My heart's desire," Ricardo repeated slowly. "As it happens, good sir, I am in love. My heart's desire is the King's youngest daughter — the lovely Princess Blanca."

The Devil flicked his tail. "Nothing could be simpler than to get her for you," he answered contemptuously.

"And how," Ricardo asked, "do you propose to manage it?"

The Devil beat his tiny fists impatiently against the glass.

"Let me out of this bottle," he snarled, "and I will manage it with no trouble at all."

But Ricardo was not a soldier of fortune for nothing.

"There is no hurry," he said mildly. "Tell me first just exactly how you propose to get the Princess Blanca for me."

The Devil, seeing what kind of a man he had to deal with, settled himself more comfortably in his bottle and unfolded his plan. He proposed to bewitch the

Princess with a strange illness in such a way that every doctor in the country would be called to cure her.

"But no doctor will cure her but you," he said, chuckling. "I will see that the King, in desperation, offers her hand in marriage to whomever rids her of the trouble. And then you can step in and, at your command, I will go back to the place that I came from."

Ricardo did not entirely approve of this plan. He did not like to be the cause of suffering to the lovely Princess. But the Devil assured him that her pain would be brief, and he finally consented.

"And now," said the Devil, "let me out of this bottle!"

"Not so fast," Ricardo answered coolly. "There is no need for haste. Time enough when we get to the palace." And he slipped the bottle, Devil and all, into the pocket of his coat. "And you might tell me," he went on, "how you got into this fix in the first place."

So as they went down the mountain the Devil told Ricardo the story of Don Demonio and his mother-in-law, and Ricardo laughed until the sides of the mountain rang again.

It soon became known throughout the kingdom that the Princess Blanca suffered from a strange illness, and that the man who cured her would be given her hand in marriage.

From far and from near came the doctors, native and foreign, old and young, grave and gay. But no one of them succeeded in ridding the Princess of her trouble.

Finally Ricardo presented himself at the Palace. And a fine figure he made, in his black suit and black cape with a black velvet cap set on his curly hair.

In an upper room of the Palace the Princess Blanca lay on her bed with closed eyes and a face as white as a jasmine flower.

"I have come to the end of my patience," the stern old King told Ricardo. "If you cure her before sunset today, she is yours. If you fail to cure her, you will be hanged from that scaffold that is even now being built in the courtyard."

Now this was rather more than Ricardo had bargained for. But he had faith in his compact with the Devil. So he answered calmly, "Leave me alone with the Princess, and I will cure her in an hour."

The King and the attendants withdrew. Going over to the bed, Ricardo called upon the Devil to lift the spell and to go back to the place that he came from.

But there was no answer!

For three long hours Ricardo begged and pleaded,

blustered and threatened.   Once he heard a thin, mocking laugh and a tiny voice that said:

"Not so fast!   No need for hurry!"

And the Princess Blanca lay scarcely breathing, her
eyes closed, her face as white as a jasmine flower.

The sun was sinking in the west, and the old King
rapping impatiently on the door, before, like a flash, an
idea came to Ricardo.   He went to the door and
opened it, just a little.

"The Princess is almost cured," he whispered to the
anxious group waiting outside.   "Tell them quickly to

ring all the bells of every church in the city to celebrate. It will please her."

The King gave the order, and in a short time the air was filled with the clamor of church bells, ringing joyously, a sound that no devil approves.

Out from behind Blanca's pillow popped a small, black head with horns, and a harsh, impatient voice demanded:

"What is all that noise about?"

And then Ricardo made his master stroke.

"That noise," he answered deliberately, "is the sound of the church bells ringing to celebrate the arrival in Granada of old Tía Pía, your mother-in-law."

With a bellow of mingled rage and fear the Devil leaped to the window and was gone, leaving behind him a strong smell of brimstone. While on the bed the color returned to the face of the Princess Blanca and her gray eyes opened to look, first with wonder and then with shy approval, at Ricardo.

And did old Tía Pía ever know that it was she and none other who had brought happiness to Ricardo and the Princess Blanca?

Probably not. But to the end of her days she chuckled with satisfaction whenever she thought of the part she had played as Don Demonio's mother-in-law.

THE SHEPHERD WHO LAUGHED LAST

THE SHEPHERD WHO LAUGHED LAST

THE landlord of the little roadside Inn near La Granja loved a good laugh.

He and his special cronies among the men who came often to the Inn never tired of repeating a funny story, or of playing a practical joke upon those who came their way. The Inn became famous for its good cheer, and it was well known that it needed a sharp wit to get the best of old Tomás, the landlord.

One night there came to the Inn a shepherd. He
was a simple looking fellow, with mild gray eyes and a
face as smooth and innocent as a babe's. And how was
Tomás to know that behind those mild eyes there was
a quick brain?

After he had served the shepherd, Tomás winked at
his cronies.

"Here is one who will be easy to fool," he whispered.

The others watched delightedly as Tomás, settling
himself comfortably before the charcoal fire and lighting his pipe, said to the stranger:

"Here in La Granja, you know, we have different
names for things. You had best learn them before you
go any farther."

The shepherd took another sip of his *valdepeñas*.

"Yes," he said stupidly.

Tomás nodded. "Yes," he answered. "Here in La
Granja we call a bottle, for example, a Fat Boy. The
blood pudding we call Johnny. The rooster we call
the Singer, the hen the Woman, the cat Our Neighbor,
the chimney chain Forbearance. We call the bed St.
Sebastian, the fire Happiness, and the master of the
house Holy Lord."

The shepherd began earnestly to repeat the new

names over and over, while the men rocked with silent laughter over his gullibility.

They were still laughing and the shepherd was still gravely conning over the names when the Inn closed for the night. Tomás went upstairs to bed, and the shepherd laid himself down beside the fire to sleep. He kept one eye open, however, and when the black cat came in he watched her. She went over to the fire for warmth and, getting too near it, set fire to the end of her tail. The pain maddened her, and yowling loudly, she began to climb up the chain into the chimney.

The shepherd rose, took a bottle or two of *valdepeñas* and the blood pudding from the cupboard, the hen and the rooster from their corner, and thrust them into his pouch.

Then he lifted up his voice and called out:

"Arise, Holy Lord, from the heights of St. Sebastian. For there goes Our Neighbor up Forbearance pursued by Happiness. As for the Fat Boys, Johnny the Singer, and the Woman, they go along the road with me!"

"What can the simpleton be saying?" Tomás thought. Then he turned over and went to sleep again.

And the shepherd unlatched the door and went off along the road, laughing.

THE GOLDEN PARROT

THE GOLDEN PARROT

IN THE old harbor city of Cádiz there once lived a rich merchant whose name was Carlos Álvarez. His house, with its high cool rooms and flower filled patio, stood just back of the quay. From his windows he could see his tall ships come in, laden with precious cargo — silks and furs, and spices, rare medicines from the East, and wrought gold and silver.

Now Don Carlos had three sons of whom he was exceedingly proud. The first, Luis, was as straight as an arrow. The second, Rodrigo, was as strong as an ox. And the third, Fernando, was so clever and so handsome that there was not in all Spain a youth to compare with him.

One day Luis, the oldest son, came to his father and said:

"Father, give me a ship with silken sails and let me sail across the seas and seek adventure."

Don Carlos agreed and in a short time the ship was ready. It was a fine sight, too, lying there in the harbor, with its narrow prow and tall masts, its glistening sails of silk, dyed purple and red, jade-green and gold. Luis bade farewell to Don Carlos and his brothers, and that night the sails of his tall ship disappeared beyond the horizon.

Now, after a certain time, Luis came to a city that was built on an island. The tall towers, the busy streets and green gardens attracted him, so he left his ship in the harbor and put up at an Inn. On the second day he walked to the Palace of the King and saw on the gate a sign that said:

THE KING'S YOUNGEST DAUGHTER, THE WISE AND BEAUTIFUL PRINCESS FLORINDA, IS HIDDEN IN THIS PALACE. WHATEVER MAN FINDS HER SHALL HAVE HER FOR HIS WIFE.

Luis read the sign, and his heart beat faster. To marry a wise and beautiful princess! Surely that would be a fitting act for the oldest son of Don Carlos Álvarez of Cádiz. He rang the bell and was admitted to the King's audience chamber.

Now the King was an old man, and was very kind hearted. And when he saw Luis, so young and straight and eager, he shook his head.

"You will never find her," he said. "Many others before you have tried and failed. And if you do not find her, you will be shut up in the deepest depths of my palace and will never see the light of the sun again."

"How much time will you give me for the search?" Luis asked.

"Three days," the King answered. "If at sunset on the third day you have not found her, you will be locked away in the dark."

For three days and two nights Luis searched the great palace. But at sunset on the third day not a trace of the Princess had he found. So he was taken to a cave of hollowed rock deep under the foundations and there locked away from the light of the sun. And in the harbor his tall ship lay, her silken sails furled.

Now as time went by and Luis did not return, Rodrigo, the second son, went to his father and said:

"Father, fit out for me a silver ship, and let me go in search of my brother."

Don Carlos, with some reluctance, agreed. And in a few weeks time a silver ship was lying in the harbor of Cádiz, riding the waters as gracefully as a silver swan.

With his father's blessing and the farewell of the household in his ears, Rodrigo sailed away as Luis had sailed before him. And in due time he came to the island city, and read the sign on the palace gate. Straightway he asked to be shown before the King.

"I am the second son of Don Carlos Álvarez of Cádiz," he said. "In the harbor here there lies a ship that I know belongs to my brother, Luis. If he has sought the Princess and failed to find her, I would seek her now in my turn. And perhaps in my search I shall find some trace of him."

The old King, moved by his strength and his good looks, begged him not to try. But Rodrigo was firm. The next day at dawn he began his quest. And for three days and two nights he hunted through every nook and corner of the great palace — and found nothing. He admitted his failure to the King and he, too, was shut in the cave away from the light of the sun.

The weeks went by, and in Cádiz, Don Carlos grieved

for his two sons. Finally Fernando, the youngest son, came to him.

"Father," he said, "there is but one thing for me to do. Fit out for me a ship of gold, and let me go and find my brothers."

At first Don Carlos refused. But he was a wise and brave man, and he knew that there would be no peace in his house until the puzzle was solved. So he fitted out a ship of gold that was a marvel to all who saw it. And, with his father's blessing in his ears and his mother's tears on his face, Fernando sailed away as his two brothers had sailed before him.

No sooner had he anchored in the harbor of the island city than he saw the silver ship and the ship with the silken sails. He went to the Palace and read the sign. But he did not at once seek the King. Instead he put up at an Inn, and taking a basket, went to the market to buy some food.

Now at one of the market stalls there sat an old woman who had cherries to sell. Fernando bought some, and as he leaned forward to pay her, she whispered in his ear:

"From your golden ship and your silver ship and your ship with the silken sails have a parrot made that stands as high as a man. Get inside the parrot and have it placed before the Palace gate. The rest will follow."

Fernando looked at her in wonder. But the old woman paid no more attention to him. She went on calling her cherries as though he no longer existed.

Fernando thought the matter over, and finally determined to take the strange old woman's advice. He hired men to break the three ships into pieces, and for many weeks the gold and silver smiths of the island city labored to make the great parrot. And a fine bird he was when he was done! He stood nearly six feet high. His body and his wings were of gold, his pedestal and his beak were of silver, and his breast and his top-knot were of many colored silk cunningly woven to simulate feathers.

In the night the golden parrot was taken to the Palace gate and Fernando crept inside, standing so that his eyes looked out of the holes that were the parrot's eyes. With him he took a flask of water and a flask of wine.

Now when the morning came, and the old King stepped out upon his balcony he saw the great, golden bird, gleaming and sparkling in the bright sun. And he was as pleased as a child. He told his servants to bring it into the Palace, and when this was done, he

They were all looking at the golden parrot

called his councillors and his chamberlains, his musicians and his pages, even the royal cook with his white cap on the back of his head and a long ladle in his hand was allowed to stand and gape at the wonderful bird. And through the eyeless sockets Fernando watched them all. And he heard every word that was said.

When night came the old King wanted the golden parrot in his bedroom. There it was placed, the King climbed into the royal bed, and the lights were put out.

Now Fernando was tired of standing in one position for so long, so, when he heard the King's gentle snores, he slipped out of the parrot and concealing himself well behind the pedestal, he stretched out on the floor and went to sleep.

He woke to the sound of voices. The royal bed-chamber was lighted again, the old King was sitting up in bed looking pleased and excited, and at the foot of the bed there stood three maidens who were all so beautiful that Fernando could hardly credit his eyesight. The first was as tall and as fair and as proud as a lily, the second as fresh and as dainty as a rose, and the third as vivid and as lovely as a pomegranate flower. And they were all engaged in looking at and exclaiming over the golden parrot.

"Ah, do let the guards carry it down to our patio,"
they pleaded.

The King begged them to wait until morning, but
they wanted it done at once. And what can one old
man do, even if he is a King, against three such lovely
maidens? Finally he clapped his hands and summoned
his two trusted guards who waited always just outside
his door. Fernando slipped back into the parrot and
watched in wonder all that followed.

First the guards moved aside the royal bed. Then
they drew up the rug, the very rug on which Fernando
had slept, disclosing a large trap door. This they
opened by pulling at an iron ring. Leading down
from the door was a flight of wide, white marble steps.
Lifting the parrot between them, with some difficulty,
the guards descended the steps, followed by the old
King wrapped in a royal purple dressing gown, and
the three maidens. At the foot of the steps there was a
large patio. It was filled with flowers and fruit trees
among whose leaves tall candles burned. Through
this patio they went, down a long corridor and into a
second and even larger patio. Orange and pomegranate trees blossomed there, roses and lilies and carnations bloomed, and in the light of a thousand wax
candles, fountains threw up their sparkling jets of

water. At the farther end were three alcoves, sepa-
rated from the patio by pointed arches, and in each
alcove was a low couch covered with velvet, one rose,
one blue and one gold.

The guards set the golden parrot down directly in
front of the alcoves. Then they and the old King went
away. The three Princesses settled themselves on their
couches, and the attendants went around the patio snuf-
fing out the candles until the whole place was in utter
darkness.

Fernando slipped out of the parrot and stood there
thinking deeply. Somehow he must get out of the
patio. He must come back to the Palace in the morning and find and claim the youngest Princess. But
which was the youngest Princess — the one as fair as a
lily, the one as fresh as a rose, or the one as vivid as a
pomegranate flower? And how could he get out of
the patio when the King himself slept over the trap
door? Could there be some other exit? Cautiously
he began to feel his way around the walls. It was
black as pitch and he was continually running into the
trees. Suddenly he felt a soft, cool hand close around
his wrist. Fernando was so startled that he nearly
cried out, but a swift "Hush!" silenced him. Guided
by the hand he was led forward into the darkness. He

heard a door open and close and felt his feet take him up and up an inclined road — up and up and up until he saw ahead of him very dimly a gate of wrought iron. Beyond it was the faint, gray light of dawn.

The shadowy figure by his side was surely one of the three Princesses. But, keenly as he looked at her, Fernando could not tell which one. She was wrapped in a long, loose robe and a heavy veil was drawn over her head and face. She drew a great iron key from her robe and unlocked the gate.

"Go!" she whispered.

But Fernando was far from satisfied.

"Tell me," he begged, "how did you know that I was there?"

Behind the veil he thought he saw the gleam of her eyes.

"I saw you in my father's room, lying behind the pedestal. And I felt your eyes looking at me through the parrot's eyes. No one else saw. And now, go quickly, but come back tomorrow."

Fernando caught one of her hands and held it as she tried to push him through the gate.

"Tell me," he demanded, "how shall I know the youngest Princess?"

She laughed softly. "Choose the one who wears a

pomegranate flower in her hair," she answered.
"Adiós!"

The next day at noon Fernando presented himself at
the Palace, and the old King shook his head more sadly
than ever when he saw him.

"There have been two fine youths before you," he
said, "and they are both shut away from the light of the
sun forever. Would you join them?"

"I want the Princess," Fernando answered boldly.
He was resolved to say nothing yet about his brothers.

The King sighed. "Very well," he said. "You may
have just three days for the search."

But the search took Fernando hardly as many minutes. To the amazement of the guards, he went straight
to the royal bedchamber and drew aside the royal bed.
Their cries of astonishment drew the King and most
of the household. And by the time Fernando entered
the second patio he was followed by a procession — the
King, his councillors, his chamberlains, the royal musicians and pages, the Court storytellers, the kitchen
maids, and even the fat cook himself with his dripping
ladle and his high white cap on one side of his head.

The three Princesses sat at their embroidery in the
soft light of the thousand candles.

The one who was as fair as a lily, and the one who

was as dainty as a rose, looked up as they came in. But the one who was as vivid as a pomegranate flower sat with downcast eyes. Fernando looked at the blossom in her hair. Then he dropped on one knee at her feet, and said clearly,

"I claim the youngest Princess!"

In his heart the old King was glad to free Luis and Rodrigo. And in a short time, three weddings, not one, were celebrated in the island city. Don Carlos Álvarez of Cádiz came to them in a tall ship. And in the wedding procession, carried high on the shoulders of the King's guards, was the Golden Parrot.

THE TINKER AND THE GHOST

THE TINKER AND THE GHOST

O N THE wide plain not far from the city of Toledo there once stood a great gray Castle. For many years before this story begins no one had dwelt there, because the Castle was haunted. There was no living soul within its walls, and yet on almost every night in the year a thin, sad voice moaned and wept and wailed through the huge, empty rooms. And on all Hallow's Eve a ghostly light appeared in the chimney, a light that flared and died and flared again against the dark sky.

Learned doctors and brave adventurers had tried to exorcise the ghost. And the next morning they had been found in the great hall of the Castle, sitting life- less before the empty fireplace.

Now one day in late October there came to the little village that nestled around the Castle walls a brave and jolly tinker whose name was Esteban. And while he sat in the market place mending the pots and pans the good wives told him about the haunted Castle. It was All Hallow's Eve, they said, and if he would wait until nightfall he could see the strange, ghostly light flare up from the chimney. He might, if he dared go near enough, hear the thin, sad voice echo through the silent rooms.

"If I dare!" Esteban repeated scornfully. "You must know, good wives, that I — Esteban — fear nothing, neither ghost nor human. I will gladly sleep in the Castle tonight, and keep this dismal spirit company."

The good wives looked at him in amazement. Did Esteban know that if he succeeded in banishing the ghost the owner of the Castle would give him a thousand gold *reales?*

Esteban chuckled. If that was how matters stood, he would go to the Castle at nightfall and do his best to get rid of the thing that haunted it. But he was a man who liked plenty to eat and drink and a fire to keep him company. They must bring to him a load of faggots, a side of bacon, a flask of wine, a dozen fresh eggs and a frying pan. This the good wives gladly did. And as the dusk fell, Esteban loaded these things on the donkey's back and set out for the Castle. And you may be very sure that not one of the village people went very far along the way with him!

It was a dark night with a chill wind blowing and a hint of rain in the air. Esteban unsaddled his donkey and set him to graze on the short grass of the deserted courtyard. Then he carried his food and his faggots into the great hall. It was dark as pitch there. Bats beat their soft wings in his face, and the air felt cold and musty. He lost no time in piling some of his faggots in one corner of the huge stone fireplace and in lighting them. As the red and golden flames leaped up the chimney Esteban rubbed his hands. Then he settled himself comfortably on the hearth.

"*That* is the thing to keep off both cold and fear," he said.

Carefully slicing some bacon he laid it in the pan and set it over the flames. How good it smelled! And how cheerful the sound of its crisp sizzling!

He had just lifted his flask to take a deep drink of the good wine when down the chimney there came a voice — a thin, sad voice — and "*Oh me!*" it wailed, "*Oh me! Oh me!*"

Esteban swallowed the wine and set the flask carefully down beside him.

"Not a very cheerful greeting, my friend," he said, as he moved the bacon on the pan so that it should be equally brown in all its parts. "But bearable to a man who is used to the braying of his donkey."

And, *"Oh me!"* sobbed the voice. *"Oh me! Oh me!"*

Esteban lifted the bacon carefully from the hot fat and laid it on a bit of brown paper to drain. Then he broke an egg into the frying pan. As he gently shook the pan so that the edges of his egg should be crisp and brown and the yolk soft, the voice came again. Only this time it was shrill and frightened.

"Look out below," it called. *"I'm falling!"*

"All right," answered Esteban, "only don't fall into the frying pan."

With that there was a thump, and there on the hearth lay a man's leg! It was a good leg enough and it was clothed in the half of a pair of brown corduroy trousers.

Esteban ate his egg, a piece of bacon and drank again from the flask of wine. The wind howled around the Castle and the rain beat against the windows.

Then, *"Look out below,"* called the voice sharply. *"I'm falling!"*

It was a good head with thick black hair

There was a thump, and on the hearth there lay a second leg, just like the first!

Esteban moved it away from the fire and piled on more faggots. Then he warmed the fat in the frying pan and broke into it a second egg.

And, *"Look out below!"* roared the voice. And now it was no longer thin, but strong and lusty. *"Look out below! I'm falling!"*

"Fall away," Esteban answered cheerfully. "Only don't spill my egg."

There was a thump, heavier than the first two, and on the hearth there lay a trunk. It was clothed in a blue shirt and a brown corduroy coat.

Esteban was eating his third egg and the last of the cooked bacon when the voice called again, and down fell first one arm and then the other.

"Now," thought Esteban, as he put the frying pan on the fire and began to cook more bacon. "Now there is only the head. I confess that I am rather curious to see the head."

And: "LOOK OUT BELOW!" thundered the voice. "I'M FALLING—FALLING!"

And down the chimney there came tumbling a head!

It was a good head enough, with thick black hair, a long black beard and dark eyes that looked a little strained and anxious. Esteban's bacon was only half cooked. Nevertheless, he removed the pan from the fire and laid it on the hearth. And it is a good thing that he did, because before his eyes the parts of the body joined together, and a living man — or his ghost — stood before him! And *that* was a sight that might have startled Esteban into burning his fingers with the bacon fat.

"Good evening," said Esteban. "Will you have an egg and a bit of bacon?"

"No, I want no food," the ghost answered. "But I will tell you this, right here and now. You are the only man, out of all those who have come to the Castle, to stay here until I could get my body together again. The others died of sheer fright before I was half finished."

"That is because they did not have sense enough to bring food and fire with them," Esteban replied coolly. And he turned back to his frying pan.

"Wait a minute!" pleaded the ghost. "If you will help me a bit more, you will save my soul and get me into the Kingdom of Heaven. Out in the Courtyard, under a cypress tree, there are buried three bags — one of copper coins, one of silver coins, and one of gold coins. I stole them from some thieves and brought them here to the Castle to hide. But no sooner did I have them buried than the thieves overtook me, murdered me and cut my body into pieces. But they did not find the coins. Now you come with me and dig them up. Give the copper coins to the Church, the silver coins to the poor, and keep the gold coins for yourself. Then I will have expiated my sins and can go to the Kingdom of Heaven."

This suited Esteban. So he went out into the courtyard with the ghost. And you should have heard how the donkey brayed when he saw them!

When they reached the cypress tree in a corner of the courtyard: "Dig," said the ghost.

"Dig yourself," answered Esteban.

So the ghost dug, and after a time the three bags of money appeared.

"Now will you promise to do just what I asked you to do?" asked the ghost.

"Yes, I promise," Esteban answered.

"Then," said the Ghost, "strip my garments from me."

This Esteban did, and instantly the ghost disappeared, leaving his clothes lying there on the short grass of the courtyard. It went straight up to Heaven and knocked on the Gate. St. Peter opened it, and when the spirit explained that he had expiated his sins, gave him a cordial welcome.

Esteban carried the coins into the great hall of the castle, fried and ate another egg and then went peacefully to sleep before the fire.

The next morning when the village people came to carry away Esteban's body, they found him making an omelette out of the last of the fresh eggs.

"Are you alive?" they gasped.

"I am," Esteban answered. "And the food and the faggots lasted through very nicely. Now I will go to the owner of the Castle and collect my thousand gold *reales*. The ghost has gone for good and all. You will find his clothes lying out in the courtyard."

And before their astonished eyes he loaded the bags of coins on the donkey's back and departed.

First he collected the thousand gold *reales* from the grateful lord of the Castle. Then he returned to Toledo, gave the copper coins to the *cura* of his church, and faithfully distributed the silver ones among the poor. And on the thousand *reales* and the golden coins he lived in idleness and a great contentment for many years.

THE GOATHERD WHO WON
A PRINCESS

THE GOATHERD WHO WON
A PRINCESS

MANUEL was a goatherd who lived in a little village not far from Seville.

Every morning he drove his goats, black and brown and gray, up the sloping hillside, past the olive grove to the pasture where they could crop the short grass. Every evening he drove them home again, chuckling often at the awkward gambols of the little kids.

Manuel was fond of his goats.   But the days were long and dull, and he pined for adventure.

One evening, when the herd had been driven into the fold, Manuel walked to the village Inn, and seating himself comfortably on the doorstep, listened to the talk that was going on about him.   It was all of the King's youngest daughter, the pretty little Princess María Cristina.   For she was a little lady who loved good stories, and she had said that she would not marry until she found a man who could tell a better story than she could tell herself.

Now the Princess María Cristina was famous for her wit and her clever tongue.   From the youngest page in the Palace to the oldest and wisest Minister of State, no one could help but listen when she told one of her tales.   With her keen wit and her fertile imagination, she put the regular Court storytellers to shame.

All this was known to Manuel, and as he listened to the latest and boldest announcement of the Princess he made up his mind to try his hand at outwitting her himself.

So the next day being a feast-day, Manuel put on his best corduroy suit with the bright silver buttons, tied a scarlet kerchief around his neck, and with his broad-brimmed hat cocked jauntily on his curly hair, set out for Seville.

The sun was low in the sky when he arrived at the King's Palace. The cypress trees in the royal garden stood dark against the rosy glow in the west. Boldly, although his heart was in his mouth, Manuel asked to be taken to the Princess. At first the guards laughed at him, but there was something in the set of his head, in the merry twinkle of his eyes, that won them over.

"Why not?" they said. "He looks as though he could tell a good story."

Through a great courtyard, down a long passage-way and into the light and color of the royal garden they led Manuel. The little Princess sat with her ladies in the shade of an orange tree. A fountain played beside her and on the grass at her feet the white and crimson petals of roses dropped, one by one.

The Captain of the Guards bowed low before her. 'Your Highness," he said, "we bring you a young goatherd who swears that he can tell a better story than Your Highness can."

María Cristina looked up at Manuel with eyes as dark and merry as his own.

"Let him try," she said. And she folded her two small hands demurely in her lap.

Manuel drew a deep breath.

"Your Highness," he began. "I have come to tell you of my travels. For I have travelled far and have had many adventures."

"And where have your travels taken you?" asked the Princess. Her voice was grave, but her eyes twinkled and there was a curve to her mouth that was a challenge to Manuel.

He straightened his shoulders and drew another long breath.

"My first trip was like this," he said. "I planted a palm tree. It grew so fast and so high that, seated in its fronds, I was taken straight up to Heaven. I arrived there just in time for the wedding of the Eleven Thousand Virgins, and because I looked at one of them with admiration, St. Peter took me by the collar and threw me outside.

"I fell without drawing a breath for a long time and finally landed on the moon. I went straight through the eye of the moon and I saw that she had hair of silver and brains of gold. I caught hold of one of the hairs. The moon saw me and promptly bit off the hair that I was hanging to. I fell and landed on earth and hid myself in a large gourd.

"There I lived comfortably until the peasants took

my house to market and sold it to a convent. The nuns thought I was a worm and threw me out into the garden. A heavy shower fell and I found that I had taken root and was growing there. I put my hand in my pocket, took out my knife and cut the roots. It did not hurt me, Your Highness. I then climbed the garden wall and walked along the road until I came to a river.

"A net lay on the bank so I tried fishing for a while and finally caught a donkey . . . a fine beast. I got on its back and rode along, passing merry jests with everyone I met. That night I noticed that there was a sore on the donkey's back. So I took him to a veterinary who told me that the only cure was to cover the sore with fresh beans. This I did, and there grew up a great forest of cork trees. I went hunting in the forest with my gun and killed a wild boar.

"I then noticed a large turtle moving rapidly along the path. I jumped on its back and it took me to the deepest depths of the sea. I found myself in a convent where the nuns were all sardines and the prioress was a whale. She promptly swallowed me. I was fairly comfortable inside, but she swam along the shore and finally cast me up near Cádiz.

"There some sailors found me, and as I was all caked with salt, they sold me to a salt merchant. He, in turn, sold me to a wealthy Sevillian nobleman who thought I was an antique statue that had been cast up by the waves of the sea. He placed me in his patio, surrounded with potted plants, fountains and fruit trees. There I stayed for some time.

"One night it rained and all the salt was washed off me. I blew on the gate of the patio and it opened and let me through. I heard that Your Highness liked a good story, so I hastened to come to Seville. And that is my first adventure."

The little Princess clapped her hands. Then she threw back her head and laughed.

"You are the man for me," she said. "And I will marry none other."

So Manuel and the Princess María Cristina were married. And they spent the rest of their lives telling one another tall tales.

THE SILVER FLUTE

THE SILVER FLUTE

O N THE lower slopes of the Sierra Nevada there once lived a man who had one son. His wife had died when the boy was a baby and the man had recently married again. Now the new wife found Jaime a nuisance and tried her best to get rid of him. His work it was to guard the sheep, to take them every day to the higher slopes of the mountain where they could find pasture. But in spite of his care and the watchfulness of his clever dog, Toro, the wolves who infested the mountains often managed to carry off a baby lamb. And then the stepmother would scold Jaime in her shrill voice and threaten to turn him out of the house.

One day in the fall when Jaime and Toro were up on the mountain with the sheep a heavy storm blew up. From the piled black clouds snow fell thickly, and a cold wind blew the flakes before it. In vain Jaime and Toro tried to round the sheep up and bring them into the shelter of the rocks. The silly things ran out into the thick of the storm, bleating pitifully. In no time at all they were scattered. Only two out of the whole flock could be found.

Jaime was in despair. When the force of the storm lessened he and Toro sought all through the upland pasture for the sheep. But not one did they find. The westering sun broke through the clouds and cast a golden light on the snow. Jaime sat down on a rock and hid his face in his hands, while Toro crouched before him, his tongue hanging out of his mouth, his eyes puzzled and anxious.

Suddenly Toro growled, and Jaime looked up. There before him stood a tall old woman. She was dressed as the peasants dress, with a black kerchief folded on her breast and another over her hair. Her eyes were gray and keen, her back as straight as an arrow, and in her face was a beauty that even age could not dim.

"You are in trouble," she said. Jaime got to his feet.

"I have lost my sheep," he answered.

The old woman put her hand into the pocket of her dress and took out a small silver flute. It was of exquisite workmanship, and at the end were carved two tiny pomegranate flowers — the ancient symbol of Granada. For a little space of time she stood looking down at the flute. Then she thrust it into Jaime's hand, and turning she disappeared around a crevice in the rock.

Jaime looked at the flute with delight. He loved music and had always longed to make it, but he had never had anything to make it with. Eagerly he put the silver flute to his lips and began to play. The notes were as full and sweet as the song of a nightingale. The tune that he played he had never even heard. It came with no effort of his will. It flowed from the flute as easily as the wind blows over the snow-covered crests of the mountains, as the cold white water flows down their flanks. It was a gay, lilting tune with a marked rhythm.

As Jaime played, he became conscious of movement about him. Looking up, he saw that the sheep had all

returned and that they were dancing! Reared up on
their hind legs, their absurd tails wagging briskly, their
long faces as solemn as owls, they were dancing around
the upland pasture, the rams and the ewes and even the
little baby lambs. And Toro was dancing with them.
His plumy tail wagging, his ears cocked, his eyes merry,

he was retreating and advancing, twirling and pirouetting in the intricate measures of the dance.

Jaime took the flute from his lips and broke into a
peal of laughter.

Instantly Toro threw himself down panting at his

feet and the sheep, getting down on all fours, began soberly to crop the grass.

After that Jaime and his sheep made merry every day on the upland pasture. The sheep danced so much, in fact, that they grew exceedingly thin. His step-mother, seeing it, scolded him roundly. But her shrill nagging voice no longer had power to hurt Jaime. He had determined to take Toro and his flute and to go out into the world and seek his fortune. His father must know first, then he would go. The stepmother sensed this new independence in him, and it made her hate him more than ever.

One evening her anger broke all bounds. As Jaime came into the kitchen for his supper, she snatched a great copper pot filled with boiling water from the fire intending to throw it at him. Jaime took his flute from where it was hidden under his coat, and began to play. And, with the pot of boiling water still in her hands his stepmother began to dance! Round and round the kitchen she went. The water splashed all over her, and she howled with pain, but she could not drop the copper pot and she could not stop dancing. Such a noise as she made! Her husband and the neigh-bors came running, men and women and children, and the instant that they came within sound of the flute, they too began to dance. Jaime stepped out upon the terrace and went on playing, faster and clearer and louder. He started to walk along the road that led to the mountains, and, willy-nilly, they were after him, advancing and retreating, whirling and pirouetting in the intricate measures of the dance!

On the road was the parish church, and the *cura* himself stood on the steps. As soon as the notes of the flute reached him, he too began to dance. And a comical figure he made, his wide brimmed hat bobbing on his head, his long robes flapping like a crow's wings. Straight toward the mountains Jaime led them, and one and all, they followed him. They might wring their hands and beg for mercy, but as long as he played, they must dance.

And, for all I know, Jaime is playing and they are dancing still.

BLACK MAGIC

BLACK MAGIC

IN A certain village near La Granja in the Asturias, there once lived a widow who had one son. Now Benito had never been as strong and active as other boys of his age, but he was keen of mind. His mother encouraged him in his studies with the village *cura,* and was very proud of his progress. By the time Benito reached his teens, he was well on the way to become a great scholar.

"Benito," said his mother to him on the morning of

his eighteenth birthday, "what is it that you want to do with all this knowledge that you have stored in your head, as the hay is stored under the thatch at harvest time?"

"Mother," Benito answered promptly, "I want to learn Black Magic."

Now in nearby La Granja there lived a famous magician. Benito had seen him once at the annual Fair. He had watched, half in fear and half in admiration, the magician's lined, forbidding face and his quiet manner as he dealt with the shopkeepers at the stalls. And he longed to be like him. So he and his mother travelled the white road to La Granja. There in his shady patio they found the magician and begged him to take Benito as a pupil.

The tall, strange old man studied Benito for a moment.

"Yes," he said at last, "I will take him as a pupil on one condition. You must leave him entirely to me for one whole year. At the end of the year you may come for him. But he goes with you only if you recognize him. If you fail to recognize him, he stays forever with me."

Benito's mother was reluctant to do this, but Benito begged so hard that she finally consented.

For one whole year, through spring and summer, through autumn and winter, Benito studied the magic arts. The great leather-bound books with their brass clasps that stood on his master's shelves had no secrets from him. His quick mind soon found the heart of the mystery, and by the New Year he knew as much about Black Magic as the great magician — and more.

Early on the morning of New Year's Day Benito flew in the form of a dove to his mother's house. He found her at the fountain scouring her copper pots.

"Listen, Mother," he said, resuming his own form. "When you come today to my master's house to get me, he will show you a flock of doves. I shall be among them, and you can pick me out from the rest because I shall fly above them as they peck at the corn. Remember that, and all will be well."

That afternoon, when the widow come to the magician's house in La Granja, he led her to the wide cool patio. There, near the central fountain, a flock of doves pecked at some scattered grains of corn. But one dove did not eat. He flew above the others, swooping and fluttering on poised white wings.

"Your son is in the patio. Do you see him?" the magician asked.

And the widow answered proudly. "My son is the

dove who flies above the others. Even as a dove, he must show that he is cleverer than others, in both his work and his play."

The magician frowned and his deep-set eyes flashed. He was obliged to keep his promise and let Benito go. But he was very angry, and in one way he was frightened. Could it be that the pupil had outstripped the master, and that Benito knew more of Black Magic than he? He made up his mind then and there he would watch and wait, and in time, destroy Benito utterly.

"Now, Mother," Benito said, when they were safely home again, "let us see what Black Magic will do to earn our bread and cheese and a bottle or two of *valdepeñas*. Tomorrow I will change myself into a cow and you can take me to market and sell me. Your price must be one hundred *reales,* no more and no less. But when the money is paid, remember to take the bell from the cow's neck. Because I shall be in the bell."

So the next day the widow took the cow that was Benito to market, and sold it. And when the bargain was completed, she put the hundred *reales* and the bell from the cow's neck in her pouch and came home again. And no sooner had she untied her pouch and taken out the bell. than there stood Benito! *That* was a clever

bit of Black Magic! And what do you suppose the
farmer thought when he went to his stable and found
the cow gone?

All through the winter Benito worked and read and
thought. He kept to the patio of his home, sitting
there day after day in the pale winter sunshine. As
long as he stayed there the magician had no power to
do him harm. When spring came the hundred *reales*
had all been spent.

"We must have more money, Mother," said Benito.
"This time I shall change myself into a horse. Take
me to the spring Fair and sell me for two hundred
reales, no more and no less. But when the money is
paid remember to take off the bridle and bring it home
with you, because I shall be in the bridle."

Now the magician had been waiting patiently for
something like this to happen. No sooner did the
widow appear at the Fair, leading the horse, than he
made an offer for it. He had disguised himself so
cleverly that she did not recognize him.

"I want two hundred *reales* for the horse," she told
him.

"That is a good price," he answered. "But I will
give it to you. I have a very special reason for want-
ing this particular horse."

He counted two hundred golden coins into her hand and she put them in her pouch. Then she turned and slipped the bridle from the horse's neck.

"Stop!" the magician commanded, and his eyes flashed like the lightning in the sky. "Stop! That bridle is mine, too."

But Benito's mother shook her head.

"No," she answered firmly. "This bridle does not go with the horse. It is one that I have had for many years, and I have no intention of parting with it."

The magician began to argue with her and their loud angry voices soon brought a crowd around them. One took one side and one another. But everyone agreed that the matter should be left to the mayor to decide. The sun was low in the sky before the mayor had heard all the arguments. But in the end he judged that the bridle belonged by right of purchase to the magician. Benito's mother wept and prayed but it was of no use.

So Benito, in the form of a bridle, was taken back to the house where he had first learned Black Magic.

"Do not take the bridle from the horse," the magician told his servants that night. "Fasten him to the iron ring in the stable. Give him food and water, but leave the bridle on or it will be the worse for you."

Now the servants were kindly men, and like all

Spaniards, they liked a horse above other animals. When, in the morning, they gave the horse his oats they saw that he could not eat them comfortably with the bit in his mouth.

"Take it off," urged one of the grooms. "The poor beast cannot eat his breakfast so."

So the bridle came off.

Instantly Benito became a swallow who darted off on pointed wings into the burning blue of the sky. The magician was watching out of his window, and like a flash, he became a great brown eagle who pursued him. Their flight took them over a river, and Benito dropped and became a tiny fish who flashed deep under the surface of the water. Instantly the magician became a large fish who could swim even faster. So far his magic was stronger than Benito's. The river flowed into a forest, and Benito leaped to its banks as a greyhound who sped swiftly off among the trees. And the magician became a wild boar, fierce and strong, who followed him puffing and blowing through his red nostrils. Fleet as the greyhound was, the boar was fleeter.

Now this forest bordered the estate of a nobleman, and as Benito broke through the underbrush, he saw ahead of him the high gate of the Castle. But it was closed and locked. With a tremendous effort Benito remembered one more magic formula and changed himself into a mosquito. It was easy enough then to fly between the bars of the gate and into the patio.

There in the shadow of a cypress tree the nobleman's lovely daughter, Miranda, sat with her curly black spaniel lying on the grass at her feet. One look at her and Benito knew that the time had come to resume his own form. Even now the boar was thrusting his head against the bars of the gate. He must act quickly, or he was lost.

From the mosquito he became himself and bowed low before Miranda, who looked at him with startled eyes.

"Who are you, and why are you in my garden?" she asked.

"I throw myself upon your mercy," Benito answered quickly. "I am followed by a magician who seeks to destroy me. I have used the most of my own magic to elude him, and if you will help me, I have one more trick to draw upon. I can change myself into a ring for your finger. When the magician comes, if he threatens you, take me from your hand and throw me hard upon the tiles of the patio. I will break into a dozen pieces and the largest piece you must cover with your foot and conceal. Whatever happens you must not let him see that piece. Will you do all this for me?"

"Yes," Miranda answered. "I will do it for you gladly." Benito's youth and his courage pleased her. And she felt an added confidence in him because the spaniel at her feet had not barked at Benito. He had wagged his tail and looked up at him with friendly eyes.

Benito bowed. "Thank you," he said. Then he bowed again, and suddenly he was gone and on her finger shone a ring of gold.

It was not very long before the magician, in his own form and in a towering rage, demanded admittance at the gate of the Castle.

"Let him come in," Miranda ordered calmly.

Now the magician had come to the end of his magic. There was only one more change that he could make, and in this last form he had determined to destroy Benito completely and forever. One look at Miranda and he knew that what he sought was the ring upon her hand.

"Give me that ring," he said harshly. And he bent over her as though he intended to do her harm.

Miranda drew the ring from her hand and threw it hard against the tiles of the patio. It broke into a dozen pieces. Swiftly Miranda put her foot over the largest piece. And it is well that she was quick, because, like a flash, the magician changed himself into a

great black cock and began to eat the pieces of the ring, pecking them up, one by one, in his strong beak.

And Benito, who was the bit of gold under Miranda's foot, made his last change. He turned himself into a red fox.

Snip! Snap! And off flew the black cock's head!

The little spaniel began to bark excitedly. Miranda's anxious eyes cleared again as Benito became himself and bowed before her.

"That is the end of my old master," he said. "And now I am the greatest magician in all Spain. Will you marry me?"

"That I will," Miranda answered. "Because I like you more than a little, and I am not afraid of your magic."

So the widow's son married the nobleman's daughter. The wedding feast lasted three days and three nights, and the only magic about it was the light of the May moon and the sound of the wind in the trees.

ABOUT THE AUTHORS

RALPH STEELE BOGGS is Professor of Spanish at the University of Miami in Florida. Previous to this position he was for a number of years Professor of Spanish and folklore at the University of North Carolina. Ever since his own college days at the University of Chicago he has combined these two enthusiasms, having majored in Spanish and chosen to prepare an *Index of Spanish Folktales* for his Ph.D. dissertation. Since graduation he has taught at the University of Puerto Rico and traveled widely in Spain and France, gathering folktales firsthand both abroad and in this country. He continues to take an active part in the American Folklore Society and the Folklore section of the Modern Language Association, writing articles and lecturing on the subject.

MARY GOULD DAVIS' name is a particularly honored one in the world of children's books. She was long associated with the New York Public Library, first as an assistant and then a supervisor. She was consultant on story telling for the Metropolitan Museum of Art as well as lecturer on story telling and folklore at Pratt Institute and Columbia University; and for many years she was editor of young people's books for *The Saturday Review of Literature*. Another distinct contribution to children's literature was her assistance in the preparation of new editions of the famous *Andrew Lang Color Fairy Books*. Miss Davis died in 1956.